DISNEY'S
Aladdin
A-MAZING ALADDIN

by Alex Simmons

Illustrations by
Yakovetic and Phil Ortiz

ISBN 1-56326-251-7

CHAPTER 1

he sun shone full and bright in Agrabah. The city gleamed like a jewel in the desert.

Despite the heat, the citizens were out enjoying the day.

Prince Aladdin and Princess Jasmine arrived at the marketplace on two beautiful white horses, with palace guards behind them.

Aladdin's pet monkey, Abu, sat on Aladdin's shoulder. The Genie floated above them, like a blue balloon in a parade.

"Hellooo, Agrabah!" the Genie said in a booming voice. "What a great day to shop till you drop."

"But for me," the Genie added as he

appeared, normal size, next to Aladdin, "I have the urge for some bird's nest soup. Hong Kong, here I come."

"Will you be gone long?" Jasmine asked.

"Not unless the bird puts up a fight." With that, the Genie vanished.

"I'm glad he came back to visit us," Aladdin told Jasmine.

"So am I," Jasmine said. "And my father is so fond of playing backgammon with the Genie."

Aladdin and Jasmine dismounted from their horses and moved through the crowd of merchants and shoppers.

The guards, watching everyone with suspicion, walked behind them.

"The marketplace is so exciting," Jasmine said. "I love the smell of spices and exotic fruits, and — "

"Fish!" cried one of the merchants. He dangled a mullet in Jasmine's face.

Abu tried to grab it, but missed.

Aladdin grinned, and they moved around the eager merchant. "We first met in the marketplace," he reminded Jasmine. "You were disguised as a peasant and —"

"How could I know that giving an apple to a hungry child could lead to such trouble?" Jasmine said. "But you came to my rescue."

"At your service," Aladdin bowed.

"I learned a valuable lesson that day," Jasmine said. She stopped by a bread cart. "To feed the hungry, one must carry money."

She picked out a loaf of bread and gave the bread merchant a gold coin.

"Oh, I don't know," Aladdin said. He puffed out his chest. "Abu and I did pretty well when we were beggars. Right, Abu?"

Abu stiffened, his eyes wide with fear.

"What's wrong?" Aladdin asked. Then he heard a low rumbling.

"The ground is moving!" Jasmine shouted.

The earth began to shake and swell. The bread cart tipped over. People screamed, dashed about, and grabbed onto anything they could to keep their balance.

Jasmine helped the bread woman. Aladdin pulled a child away from a falling wagon.

The ground split open. A crack raced toward an empty building behind the bread

cart. Steam gushed from the opening with a loud hiss and the building seemed to scream.

Then, almost as quickly as it began, the quaking stopped and the crack closed.

Abu had his arms and tail wrapped around Aladdin's head.

"It's all right now," Aladdin told him, but Abu couldn't stop trembling.

The marketplace slowly returned to normal. The merchants looked dazed as they straightened out their goods. Customers warily returned to make their purchases.

"I've never seen anything like that in Agrabah," Aladdin said.

"And I hope we won't see another for a long, long time," Jasmine said. "At least no one was hurt."

Jasmine and Aladdin continued their browsing. They didn't pay any attention to the empty building behind the bread cart and didn't see the glowing red eyes in the window.

CHAPTER 2

'm back!" the tall, thin figure said. He floated above a large crack in the floor.

With his high forehead, long black hair, and glowing red eyes, he looked like a human vulture.

"It has been such a long time." He threw open his crimson cloak and held out his arms. "One hundred years since the people knelt before the sorcery of Ben Baba Abad!"

Yellow smoke rose from the crack in the floor and swirled around Ben Baba Abad.

"It is time for me to rule Agrabah again," he whispered. With a wave of his hand he closed and sealed the crack in the floor.

"Now to meet the public." Abad pulled a hood up over his head. Moments later he moved among the people in the marketplace.

He stopped at a fruit stand. "Aha," said Abad. "This looks like a good place to start." The sign overhead read, "Daoud's Foods, Fruits and Nuts — Our Specialty."

"And two of his customers look very rich," he said. Abad was staring at Aladdin and Jasmine. He moved toward them, but stopped when Abu began to chatter at him.

"Still nervous about the ground shaking?" Aladdin asked Abu. "I know what'll make you feel better." He held up a kumquat.

"The Prince has excellent taste," said the merchant.

"A prince? How interesting," said Abad.

Abu licked his lips.

"The way to Abu's courage is through his stomach," Jasmine said.

Abu scowled but grabbed the kumquat.

Abad inched toward the fruit stall. "Now for a little fun," he said.

Abad reached out and touched a melon.

For a moment it glowed with a weird red light. Then the light faded.

"Please, please. Do not mash the fruit!" the merchant cried as he grabbed the melon. "I, Daoud Sahadi, personally carried it on my back across miles of hot, dry..." Sahadi stiffened. His eyes shimmered with the same red glow.

"Are you all right?" Jasmine asked.

Sahadi snatched a basket of dates from Jasmine. "If you are not going to buy, then do not touch."

"But I —"

"You and the Prince have disturbed my business long enough," Sahadi said.

"Sahadi, what is wrong?" Aladdin asked. "I've never seen you like this."

"Be gone!" Sahadi shouted.

Abu jumped to the awning above the fruit stall and began screeching at Sahadi.

"That is no way to talk to the Prince and Princess of Agrabah," said a woman.

"They have been more than good to us," said another.

Ben Baba Abad studied Aladdin and Jasmine. "The people love their Prince and Princess! If they were in my power..."

"If they are so wonderful, they can buy all my fruit!" Daoud Sahadi shouted. He picked up a melon and aimed it at Jasmine.

A palace guard leaped forward. The melon hit him in the face.

"Now wait a minute," Aladdin called out. But it was too late. Sahadi began throwing more of his fruit. He hit several people and suddenly everyone was throwing things.

The people were angry at Sahadi and some tried to grab him. But when they touched him, their eyes shone with a red glow. When the glow vanished, their faces seemed filled with anger and they tried to grab others.

Two of the guards jumped on Sahadi. They stiffened. Their eyes glowed with the same red light.

Abad laughed. "The Red Evil spreads and my power grows."

The guards began to fling fruit and tip over carts. As they touched others in the crowd, Abad's evil continued to spread.

Chaos ruled. Ben Baba Abad smiled. "Now for the Prince and Princess."

Aladdin pulled Jasmine away from the crowd. "People, be calm!" he called out. But no one was listening. Aladdin and Jasmine dodged the fighters and flying objects.

Abad frowned. "Luck is with them. They remain untouched."

"Where's the Genie when you need him?" Abad heard Aladdin ask Jasmine.

"June, I'm home!" the Genie appeared in a puff of blue smoke, holding a set of chopsticks. "Whoa! Talk about stressed out."

A vase flew past his head. "Did I come at a bad time?"

Ben Baba Abad's eyes grew wide. "A blue genie!" he said. "With his power, I could rule not only Agrabah but also the world!"

enie, do something!" Abad heard Jasmine shout above the noise.

"I suggest some warm milk and a good bedtime story," the Genie said. "Or maybe — "

"Genie!" Aladdin yelled. "Stop them!"

The Genie folded his arms and blinked. A black cloud appeared over the marketplace. Thunder cracked and rain poured down.

Everyone except Aladdin and Jasmine was soaked — even Abu, who glared at the Genie as he squeezed water from his hat.

"Sorry about that," the Genie told him.

"There will be no more fighting," Aladdin told the crowd.

"Especially from my palace guards," Jasmine added, and all grew quiet.

"The people still obey them," said Abad. "If only I could control the royal pair, my task would be easier. But the Genie protects them. So I must plan."

Abad studied the crowd. Their blank eyes pleased him. "A good start," he said, "but not enough." He looked at Aladdin, who was speaking to Daoud Sahadi.

"I've never seen you like this, even when I used to, uh, borrow fruit from you."

Sahadi glared at him.

Aladdin turned to Jasmine. "Let's go home. There's nothing more we can do here."

He and Jasmine mounted their horses, and Abu leaped onto Aladdin's shoulder.

"I will have them as my subjects," said Ben Baba Abad. His eyes glowed bright red, as did the eyes of the two guards under his control. They began to inch toward the Prince and Princess.

"Smells like somebody burned the biscuits," said the Genie, sniffing the air.

Abad's eyes stopped glowing and the guards stopped in their tracks. "Later," he whispered, as he shrank back into an alley.

"Come on, Genie," Aladdin said.

"Your wish is my command!" He chuckled and flew after them. "Forget I said that." Floating above their heads, Genie followed Aladdin and Jasmine back to the palace.

"So, he is the Genie's master," Ben Baba Abad said. "When I control Aladdin, I will also control that genie. The guards will infect him with the Red Evil at the palace."

Meanwhile, Ben Baba Abad slipped into the abandoned building. A few seconds later a light flashed from inside.

A sign appeared on the outside of the building. It read, "A Bad Café. Enter freely."

The door opened, haunting music filled the street, and the people began to enter.

"This is awful," the Sultan declared. Aladdin and Jasmine had just finished telling him about the fight. "There has been peace in this city for a hundred years. Except for that incident with Jafar."

Jafar had been the Sultan's vizier, the chief adviser. He had also been an evil sorcerer. When Jafar discovered Aladdin had a magic lamp with a genie, he had tried to steal it. But he had failed. Now Jafar was imprisoned in a magic lamp of his own, far out in the desert.

"What happened a hundred years ago?" Aladdin asked.

"I don't know," the Sultan said. "It's more legend than anything else."

"Perhaps the Prince and Princess should not have gone to the marketplace," said Khalid. He was the new vizier of Agrabah. "You know the people are unstable."

"That's not true!" Jasmine declared.

The Genie was floating nearby. Abu floated next to him on the Magic Carpet.

"Please say I can turn this Khalid guy into a toad," he asked Abu, who glared at Khalid, then shook his head.

"You're right," the Genie said. "Someone beat me to it."

"Cut it out, you two," said Aladdin.

"This is all very upsetting," the Sultan said. "But I have other matters of state to address."

Jasmine grabbed his arm. "Father! Wait! Some of our guards were acting strangely."

"That's right, Your Highness," Aladdin said. "They barely obeyed us and — "

"The Sultan has far more important things to tend to," said Khalid.

The Genie grew larger and floated over Khalid's head. "How does that toad spell go?"

Khalid became silent.

"Father, please do something."

The Sultan stroked his beard for a moment. "Very well," he said. "Aladdin, you are in charge of this. Look into the matter and report to me."

With that, the Sultan and Khalid left.

"Great!" Aladdin cried. "Genie, I want you and Abu to scout the town. But stay hidden."

"Wow! An undercover job." There was a puff of smoke, and a blanket covered the Genie. A periscope popped out of the top. "I'm your eye-spy guy."

Aladdin grinned. "Get back to me as soon as possible," he said. "I'm going up to Jafar's old laboratory in the tower. One of his books might have some information we could use."

"And what will I be doing?" Jasmine asked.

"Staying here and keeping an eye on those guards," Aladdin replied. "And don't worry, the Magic Carpet will guard you." The Carpet jumped to attention and saluted Aladdin.

"I am not some helpless creature you must protect, O great one!" Jasmine said angrily.

"Good time for an exit, stage right," the Genie told Abu. With a snap of his fingers, they vanished in a puff of blue smoke.

"But I was just..." Aladdin stuttered.

"And the sooner you learn that, the better." Jasmine stormed out of the hall.

"I'll be in the garden, Aziza," Jasmine said as she passed a servant. "Please bring me a drink, to cool off." Aziza bowed.

"Oh, great!" Aladdin sighed. "Watch over Jasmine," he told the Magic Carpet. "But keep out of sight. Strange things are brewing

in Agrabah."

The Magic Carpet floated off after the Princess, and Aladdin headed for Jafar's laboratory.

Aziza was on her way to the kitchen when a hand — belonging to one of the guards who had been in the marketplace — reached out from behind a pillar and grabbed her.

Aziza froze. A red light shone in her eyes. When the light faded an evil grin crossed her face.

"Who do you serve?" the guard asked.

"I serve Ben Baba Abad," Aziza replied. Her voice sounded hard and angry.

"Good," said the guard. "Now go give the Princess her drink. And be sure to hand it to her, personally."

CHAPTER 4

afar's laboratory was in the highest tower of the palace. It was a dark, eerie place filled with strange objects and shelves brimming with old books. The walls seemed saturated with evil, even though the master was gone.

Aladdin skimmed through the titles of the ancient volumes.

"Spells for a Thousand and One Tails," he read aloud. Another was entitled, *Dragons to Flies & Other Transformations.*

Aladdin continued looking until he found a newer volume: *The Darkest Tales of Agrabah.* "Maybe this will hold some answers," he said.

Aladdin had no clear idea what he was

looking for — a rumor, a name, a legend.

"This could take hours," he sighed.

But luck was with him. He found what he wanted on page twelve, in a chapter called "Old Agrabah."

"*One hundred years ago,*" Aladdin read aloud. "*Agrabah was a city of evil. It was ruled by a cruel and powerful sorcerer named Ben Baba Abad.*"

The book went on to say that the sorcerer's powers came from infecting the subjects with a spell called the Red Evil.

"*But he was finally defeated by a mighty wizard,*" Aladdin read. "*Using a golden talisman, the wizard turned Abad's own power against him.*"

Aladdin shivered. "*The spell was only temporary,*" he read. "*In one hundred years, Abad will be free again. If he can infect enough subjects with the Red Evil, he will regain all his powers. Agrabah may be lost.*"

Aladdin's mind was racing. He remembered the earthquake. He felt certain that something terrible — Ben Baba Abad — had escaped from below.

Jasmine sat in the garden, stroking Rajah, her tiger.

"Aladdin can be so pigheaded," she told Rajah. The tiger nodded. "But he can also be kind and considerate." Rajah cocked his head and stared at her.

Jasmine got up and began to pace. She walked around the large stone fountain. "Agrabah is my city, too. As the Sultan's daughter, I must face its dangers."

Jasmine scratched Rajah's head. "I know you want to protect me, Rajah. But I'm not a little girl anymore."

Aziza came into the garden. She was carrying a cool drink made from crushed almonds. Her eyes glowed with the Red Evil.

Rajah growled when Aziza approached them.

"Stop that, Rajah," Jasmine said. "You know Aziza."

"Here is your drink, Your Highness," Aziza

said. She moved closer, offering the cup.

Jasmine reached for the cup, but Rajah jumped and knocked Aziza down.

As soon as he touched Aziza, Rajah's eyes turned red and he roared.

Rajah turned toward Jasmine, his teeth flashing and his claws extended.

"Rajah, what's wrong?" cried Jasmine.

Rajah swiped at her, but Jasmine dodged to one side. She grabbed a branch and swung up into an olive tree. Rajah clawed the trunk.

Rajah roared, then moved forward.

Up in the tower, Aladdin heard Jasmine's shout. "Jasmine!" he cried, and raced from the room down the stairs.

The Magic Carpet was already on its way. It flew into the garden and headed for the Princess.

Jasmine leaped from the tree and the Carpet caught her and flew up.

"Go down," she told it. "Something is wrong with Rajah."

Again and again Jasmine and the Carpet flew past Rajah. He roared at them, but made only a feeble attempt to strike.

"He doesn't really want to hurt us," Jasmine said. "But he is angry, just like the guards."

Aladdin raced into the garden. Rajah let out a fierce growl, then shook his head.

"I think he's hurt!" Jasmine called.

Aladdin spotted a large bird cage. "Drive him toward the cage," he shouted.

Jasmine and the Carpet made Rajah back up until he had stepped inside the cage, then Aladdin slammed the door and bolted it.

Jasmine and the Carpet landed and she explained what had happened.

"Where's Aziza?" Aladdin asked.

"She must have run into the palace," Jasmine said. "What's happening?"

"I think this all has to do with an evil sorcerer," Aladdin answered. "And if we don't do something soon, Agrabah may be doomed."

CHAPTER 5

he Genie and Abu stood in a shadowy doorway in the deserted marketplace, out of the night wind.

"This place isn't going to win any tourist points with Club Ahmed," the Genie told Abu. "The folks are unfriendly, and you can't get good bottled water."

Abu glanced around toward a building across the plaza. He tugged at the Genie's sash.

"What's up, my dear Watson?" the Genie said. He was wearing a deerstalker hat and smoking a curved pipe.

Abu pointed to the building.

"I was noticing that place, too," the Genie

said. "A Bad Café. I don't think I'll be ordering the seafood." The Genie grinned. "But with the proper disguises, I'll bet we can enter and learn something about what's going on around here."

Abu scratched his head.

"What disguise?" Genie asked. "Don't worry. I'll think of something."

They walked across the plaza as the Genie and Abu winked in and out of costumes, from sailors, to peddlers, to clowns.

By the time they entered the café, they were in trench coats and fedoras. All eyes were on them. "Major bad vibes," he said as he looked around. "Either they don't like us, or the goat milk has gone sour."

The Genie and Abu moved to the center of the room. People continued to stare.

The Genie threw off his coat and hat. Now he was wearing a white tuxedo and a top hat and leaning on a cane. He leaped onto the table and a spotlight appeared out of nowhere. "Now, for my opening number…"

A flash of red light and yellow smoke

stopped the show. Abu hid under the table. When the smoke cleared, Ben Baba Abad floated above the floor in the center of the room.

"What an entrance!" the Genie said.

"I was just thinking about you," Ben Baba Abad said. He peered at Abu on the table. "And you brought a little pet, too."

Abu rolled his hands into fists and chattered angrily.

The Genie caught Abu by the shoulder. "He's mine," the Genie said. He was now wearing a cowboy outfit. "Who are you, stranger?"

"I am Abdel Rasheem Ben Baba Abad, sorcerer supreme!"

Genie raised an eyebrow. "That's easy for you to say."

Ben Baba Abad grinned.

The Genie wiggled his fingers at Ben Baba Abad. "Well, this town isn't big enough for the two of us, Benny."

"Then I guess I'll have to shrink you down to size!" Ben Baba Abad raised his hand and

fired a crimson ray at Abu.

The Genie whirled around and blocked the ray with a ball of blue light. "Oh, I'm so good!"

"Really?" Abad said.

Before the Genie could turn around again more bolts of magic flew from Abad's hands.

The Genie shrank to the size of a small frog. Abad picked him up and a red glow appeared around the Genie's small body.

"Yuck!" the Genie said, struggling against Abad's grip. "I wouldn't want to hold hands with you on a date."

"Amazing," Abad said. "My Red Evil has no effect on him."

"Better go for help, Abu. Fast!" the Genie told Abu, just as Abad shut the Genie into a gold box.

Abad fired a bolt at Abu, but the monkey leaped out of the way. He raced across the floor and in two hops was out the window.

He was trembling with fear but took to the roofs and headed toward the palace.

CHAPTER 6

grabah looks so peaceful," Jasmine said. "But I feel a horror creeping over it."

Aladdin and Jasmine were on the balcony overlooking the city. The Magic Carpet had draped itself over the railing and its tassels blew in the breeze.

"I'm sure Ben Baba Abad is behind this. Jafar's old book revealed the whole legend. Abad overcomes the good in people with his Red Evil power. One person can infect other people only by touching them, but Abad can infect people by touching them or an object they are holding. The more people he controls, the more his power grows."

"And in the old days he controlled the whole city?" Jasmine asked.

"That's right. The people, like zombies, were forced to serve him."

"But you said a wizard finally defeated him," Jasmine said.

"It was a fierce battle. The wizard's spell didn't destroy Abad, but it entombed him far below ground. The spell was only good for a hundred years. Now Ben Baba Abad is free."

"Well, we've warned my father, and we've searched the whole palace. Most of the guards and servants have disappeared, including Aziza."

"They're probably under Ben Baba Abad's spell," Aladdin said.

A tear rolled down Jasmine's cheek. "And Rajah was infected, trying to protect me."

"It's not your fault." Aladdin said.

Abu rushed into the room. Chattering wildly, he leaped onto the balcony railing and pointed toward the marketplace.

"The Genie is in trouble!" Aladdin said. "I've got to help him." The Magic Carpet rushed to his side.

"Let's see how Rajah is. Then we'll go together," Jasmine said.

But when they got to the garden they found the cage empty. "He's gone!" she cried. "Who would let him out?"

"If this is Abad's work…" Aladdin said through clenched teeth. "Carpet! Take us to the marketplace!"

They soared into the air.

"Anyone who isn't under Abad's power must be hiding," Aladdin said as they neared the empty marketplace.

Abu directed them to A Bad Café. They set down on the roof of a nearby building.

Strange music was coming from the café.

"If we go in, be sure no one touches you," Aladdin said.

"It would be better if no one could recognize us," said Jasmine.

Aladdin spotted some clothes hung out on a line to dry. "Disguises!" he said with a grin. "You remember how, don't you?"

A few minutes later, Aladdin and Jasmine

entered the café dressed in ordinary clothes. Aladdin carried the Carpet, with Abu rolled up inside.

No one in the café ate, drank, or talked; they simply sat and scowled.

"Where is everyone?" Jasmine whispered.

"Do you trust me?" Aladdin asked her. She winked. "Follow me."

Abu began thrashing inside the Carpet. "Calm down," Aladdin whispered to him. "This is the only way."

Aladdin and Jasmine boldly walked through a doorway at the back of the café, where they removed their disguises.

"It's so cold and dark in here," Jasmine said. She moved closer to Aladdin.

Aladdin sniffed the air. "Don't worry," he said. "Just be careful and we — "

The room was suddenly drenched in a red glow. The floor fell out from under them and they dropped through space, with no bottom in sight.

CHAPTER 7

e're sliding down a chu-u-u-te!" Aladdin cried out. They all yelled "Ahhhh!" as they fell.

The chute ended abruptly. Aladdin and Jasmine landed on the stone floor of a small round room. The Magic Carpet fell beside them and Abu rolled out.

"Welcome to my world!" a voice boomed. "This has been my home for one hundred years."

The ghostly image of Ben Baba Abad floated in the air. His voice seemed to come from all around them.

Aladdin noticed two tunnels that led off into deeper darkness.

"Those might be ways out," he whispered to Jasmine.

"Forgive me for not appearing in person," Abad said. "But I am entertaining guests in another part of my underground kingdom."

The walls of the room were covered with dirt and oozing with slime. Insects crept in and out of holes, and scaly things slithered along the floor.

Abu hopped onto the Magic Carpet, which floated just above the floor, trying not to touch anything.

"You should fire your housekeeper," Jasmine shouted.

Abad chuckled. "I've heard so much about you two."

"From whom?" Aladdin asked.

"Your genie," Abad replied. "Without knowing it, he's made it clear just how important you are to my plans."

"What do you mean?" said Aladdin.

"The blue genie told me you set him free," Abad said. "That's why he's too powerful for me to infect with my evil. He has a will of his own. Take back his freedom, Aladdin. Make him your slave again. Then he would be too weak to resist my power."

"But you have him in your power, don't you?" Jasmine said.

"My spell can hold him but not control him," Ben Baba Abad explained. "That is why you must put him back under your power."

"Never!" Aladdin declared.

"That's telling him, Chief!" came a voice from one of the tunnels. Aladdin couldn't tell which one.

"Genie! Where are you?" he called out.

"Ha-ha!" said Ben Baba Abad. "Your genie is down one of these tunnels."

A mighty roar echoed through the room.

"And down the other is the tiger," Abad continued. "Your palace guards brought him to me. I control almost everyone in Agrabah." Abad's voice echoed off the walls. "There is no escape. Give me the Genie and I might set you free."

"Sure you will," Aladdin muttered. He began to laugh.

"What is so funny?" Ben Baba Abad asked.

"You call yourself all-powerful," Aladdin said. "That's what's funny."

"You doubt my power?" Abad roared.

"What do you think?" Aladdin leaned against the wall. A glowing red cockroach headed for him, but he jerked away and Abu swatted it with his hat.

Aladdin smiled. "Jasmine and I gave the Genie his freedom. And what was given freely must be given back freely. You can't make us do anything."

"I don't think you want to get him angry, Al." The Genie's hollow voice sounded nervous.

Aladdin glanced at the dead cockroach. "You have to control people's minds. Otherwise they would never follow you. In fact, they would defeat you easily."

"What are you doing?" Jasmine asked. Aladdin put his finger to his lips.

"A wise ruler knows how to lead his people without using fear," Aladdin said. "Even I know how."

"You think yourself wiser than I?" Ben Baba Abad asked in a sinister voice.

"Even Abu could outwit you," Aladdin replied.

Abu jumped away and tried to roll himself up in the Magic Carpet.

"Then prove it," Abad commanded. "Free your friends by outwitting my maze. I built it while I was trapped down here."

"Nice hobby," the Genie said.

"And if we find the Genie and Rajah?" Aladdin asked. "Will you set them free?"

"Of course." Ben Baba Abad laughed. "But if you fail to complete my maze then you must give me control of the Genie."

Aladdin knew he couldn't trust Abad.

"What about the people of Agrabah?" Jasmine asked.

"Nearly all of them are already down here, paying me tribute," Abad said. "So you had better hurry."

"Why?" Aladdin asked.

"In a little while I will be at full power. And I will be ready to return to the surface —

for good. With or without your genie."

"The maze awaits you." Abad's image began to fade. "And it is filled with a number of nasty surprises." The room fell silent.

"We should split up," Jasmine said. "We'd have a better chance of finding the Genie and Rajah."

"I don't like that idea," Aladdin said.

"We have no choice." Jasmine pointed to the tunnel on the right. "I think Rajah is down this way. He won't hurt me, no matter what that sorcerer has done to him."

"Take the Magic Carpet," Aladdin said. "Abu and I will try the other tunnel."

Jasmine and Aladdin hugged each other. "Be careful," Aladdin said. He watched as the Magic Carpet followed Jasmine into the tunnel on the right.

A second later Aladdin and Abu entered the other tunnel and were lost in the dark.

CHAPTER 8

 laddin moved carefully through the tunnel with Abu on his shoulder. The passages twisted and turned, first left, then right. Flaming torches were stuck in the walls every few feet. Their flickering light cast grotesque dancing shadows.

"Genie!" Aladdin called out. "Can you hear me?"

"I sure can," the Genie replied. "But I'd rather see your smiling face."

"We'll get you out," Aladdin said. He wished he were as sure as he sounded. He was facing a blank wall. And there was no way around it. "It looks like a dead end."

"Just look out for booby traps," the Genie yelled.

"Don't worry about me," Aladdin said as he stepped back. "I can handle it." Then Aladdin froze. He had stepped on something. It felt like a small rock, but it began to sink into the floor.

Aladdin heard a rumbling sound. "I think I set off a trap!" he shouted.

"Ooops," the Genie said.

The wall slid open. Squeals and shrieks pierced Aladdin's ears. Hundreds of tiny yellow eyes glared at him. Furry gray bodies raced from the opening.

"Rats!" he shouted. Aladdin raced back the way he had come, staying just ahead of the snarling vermin.

He spotted a turn he had missed before and quickly darted down that passage.

The rats were getting closer. The passage twisted and turned this way and that. Aladdin couldn't tell if he was going in circles or not.

When the one passage split into two, Aladdin went to the left. "This must be the right way," he muttered.

Abu chattered in his ear.

The passage ended abruptly. Aladdin was on a ledge above a pit of giant scorpions. They began to climb toward him over the rock walls.

"Then again, maybe not."

Aladdin saw the entrance to another passage across the pit. He could hear the rats closing in behind him. Looking around, Aladdin spotted thick roots than ran along the wall and up to the ceiling.

He ripped a root away from the wall and, with Abu clinging to him, catapulted into space. "Hold on!" he shouted.

The root was longer than Aladdin had realized. His swing was taking them down toward the scorpions.

One uncurled its giant tail. The huge stinger glistened with poison.

Abu shut his eyes tight.

Aladdin snapped his body to the left, and they missed the stinger by inches.

They landed safely on the other side of the pit. "You weren't scared were you, buddy?"

he asked Abu.

Abu nodded.

"Me, too," Aladdin admitted. Without looking back, he and Abu raced down the passage.

Meanwhile, Jasmine and the Carpet moved along their tunnel as fast as they could.

"If I ever get out of here, I'll need to take a bath for a week." She swatted at a bug that had landed in her hair.

On the way to the bug, though, her hand struck a lever on the wall. From behind her, the sound of rushing water filled the tunnel.

"Fly, Carpet, fly!" she shouted as she jumped aboard.

They took off just as the flood covered the spot where they had been.

The ceiling was inches from her head. The Carpet had to fly low, twisting and turning as it whipped through the passages.

Just when she thought the wall of water would overtake them, they passed over a crevasse. The advancing wave dropped down into the blackness below.

"We're safe!" Jasmine said. "For now."

Jasmine and the Carpet wound farther down the passage. Twice they had to retrace their steps, only to find another dead end.

In the darkness, hairy things brushed against her face. Sometimes the walls pressed in so close that they could barely fit through. But finally, Jasmine and the Magic Carpet flew into a huge cavern.

At that moment, Aladdin and Abu came out of the passage next to her.

Aladdin rushed to her side. "Are you all right?"

"I'm fine." Jasmine hugged him. "But I see we are not alone."

A huge throne carved out of jagged rock stood in the center of the cavern. And on that throne sat Ben Baba Abad.

The people of Agrabah were kneeling around him. Aladdin saw Aziza and many of the palace guards. "You did very well," the sorcerer said. He stood up, spread his arms, and the people backed away. Rajah had been chained to the throne. A small gold box was on the floor next to him.

Abu started toward the box, but Rajah roared.

"You had Rajah here all the time," Jasmine said angrily.

"Where's the Genie?" Aladdin asked.

Ben Baba Abad grinned and slyly covered the box with his foot. "You didn't expect me to play fair, did you?"

Aladdin took a few steps forward. "And you didn't expect us to make it through your mazes, either."

Ben Baba Abad sat on the throne, keeping his foot on the box. "It makes no difference," he said. "I will tell you where the Genie is if you promise to give me control of him."

"He's not mine to give!" Aladdin shouted.

"You lie!" Baba Abad yelled. He jumped to his feet and the gold box rolled nearer Rajah. "Now, feel my power!"

"Jump on!" Aladdin shouted. He, Abu, and Jasmine leaped onto the Carpet. They sped toward the ceiling with amazing speed.

"You cannot escape me that way," Abad cried out. "I do not need your genie to rule Agrabah. Thus, I do not need you!" Abad fired a bolt of yellow light at them, then another. The Carpet evaded both bolts.

Crackling yellow and red lightning smashed against the walls and cavern floor. Large cracks began to appear and spread.

"Once Agrabah is mine, I will have power enough to control the Genie," Abad yelled. "Then the world will be mine."

Slabs of rock crashed to the ground. The people fell forward and covered their heads.

Rajah roared and pulled at his chain. One of the links snapped in two. Rajah lunged and swatted the gold box across the floor.

"Do I detect a note of hostility?" the Genie asked from the box.

"Rajah will hurt somebody if we don't do something fast," Jasmine cried.

"It's real cramped in here," the Genie called out. "I'm ready for my own house now. You know, fix the roof, paint the shutters, mow the lawn on Saturdays."

"That's the Genie's voice," Aladdin said.

Spotting the gold box, Aladdin suddenly remembered Jafar's book: *"Using a golden talisman, the wizard turned Abad's own power against him..."*

"Hold on!" Aladdin shouted. "Carpet, take me to that gold box."

Diving through a hailstorm of magic bolts, the Carpet zipped down close to the floor and Aladdin scooped up the box.

"Now, back to Ben Baba Abad!" Aladdin shouted. The Carpet changed its course and headed toward the throne.

"That's not the best idea you've ever had, Al," the Genie said from inside the box.

"Come greet your doom!" Abad cried out. He fired a red bolt straight at the Carpet.

Aladdin held the gold box in front of himself. The bolt struck the box and bounced back, striking Abad. The box flew from Aladdin's hand.

It cracked open and the Genie burst forth—full-sized. "Look out Benny — the Blue Boy's back in town!"

The Genie fired a blast at Ben Baba Abad, who had been dazed by the reflected bolt.

"Not again!" Ben Baba Abad screamed as he was swallowed by a blue ball of light.

"Where did you send him?" Aladdin asked.

"To a place with no zip code," the Genie replied proudly. He picked up Rajah and carried him to Jasmine. Rajah licked her face and purred.

"Rajah is himself again," Jasmine said, scratching him.

"I have a way with animals," the Genie said.

Suddenly there was a loud rumbling, and chunks of rock fell from the ceiling.

"Genie, the cave is collapsing! We'll be trapped!" Aladdin shouted.

"That's what happens when the landlord doesn't keep a place up," said the Genie.

People ran for cover as the walls began to fall in. But the only place to run was back to the maze.

"Can you get us out of here? All of us?"

Aladdin asked.

"You need to ask?" the Genie snapped his fingers, there was a flash, and everyone vanished, just as the cavern collapsed.

In an instant, everyone was back in the marketplace.

The earth rumbled a bit under them, then fell still. The people slowly realized they were free of the Red Evil. They began to cheer.

"I am so sorry, mistress," said Aziza. "But I could not help myself."

Daoud Sahadi raced over to Aladdin. "Oh, many, many thanks from this humble one. And also from the people of Agrabah."

"Where are the reporters?" the Genie asked. "I think we should get headline coverage. And medals, statues, maybe a few free tickets to a good show with — "

Jasmine placed a finger on the Genie's lips. "Let's go home. I want to see how my father is doing."

Aladdin, Jasmine, and Abu flew off on the Carpet. The Genie flew alongside carrying Rajah.

The people of Agrabah applauded below.

"My public." The Genie chuckled and waved back.

"Do you think we've seen the last of Ben Baba Abad?" Jasmine asked.

"I hope so," said Aladdin. "But he helped me learn a lesson."

"What?" Jasmine asked.

"As long as friends stick together, they can do anything."

"That's great," the Genie said. "Maybe we can have it printed on T-shirts. Sell them in the marketplace. Put my picture on them."

Aladdin and Jasmine stared at the Genie.

The Genie shrugged. "Then again, maybe not."

Aladdin and Jasmine began to laugh and didn't stop until they had reached the palace.